Be
yourself

LITTLE RED RHUPERT

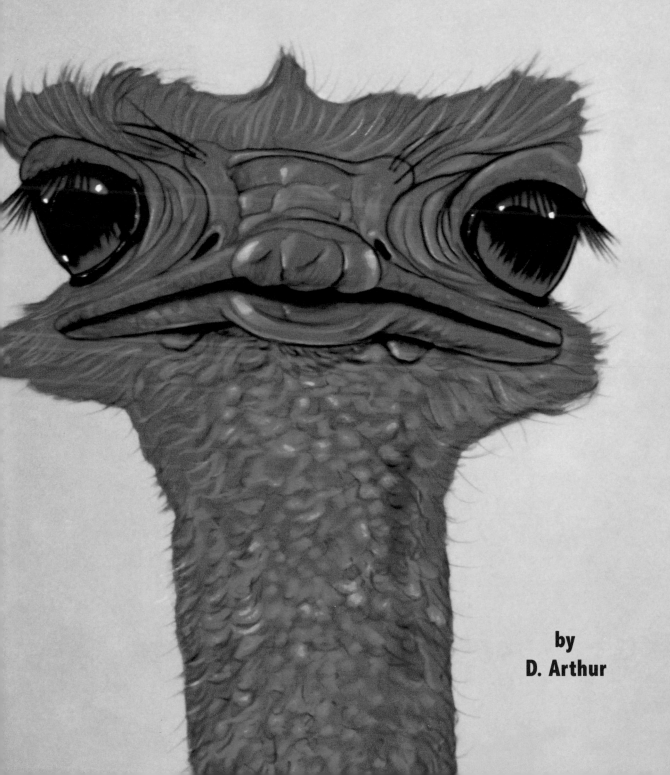

by
D. Arthur

Red Rhupert,
Red Rhupert,

WHO ARE YOU
Red Rhupert?

In the Land of Rhupert
across the Rhupert Sea,
sat Little Red Rhupert...

and RED was all he could be

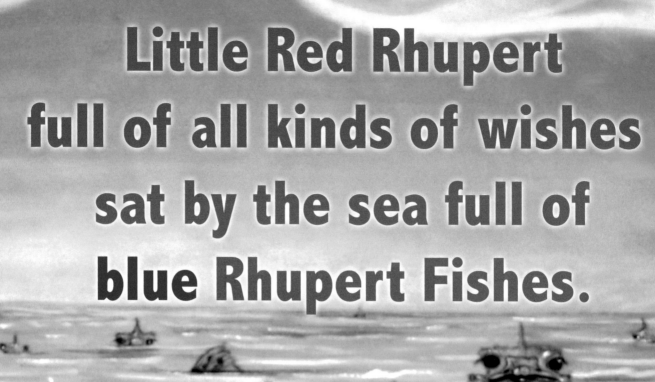

Little Red Rhupert
full of all kinds of wishes
sat by the sea full of
blue Rhupert Fishes.

Over there on the hilltop,
the brown Rhuperts live,

and

down in the valley,
the purple Rhuperts give . . .

Purple platypus kisses
to their good
purple kids.

Orange Rhuperts

are tiny and don't make a sound.
But, who could tell?
Who could tell?

They weigh barely a pound!

Pink polka-dotted Rhuperts, the **largest by far,**

They live in green Jelly Bean houses full of Jelly Bean green cats!

OH!
Red Rhupert, Red Rhupert,
WHO ARE YOU,
RED RHUPERT?

A good question to ask of the
BIG BON RED FLUGURT!

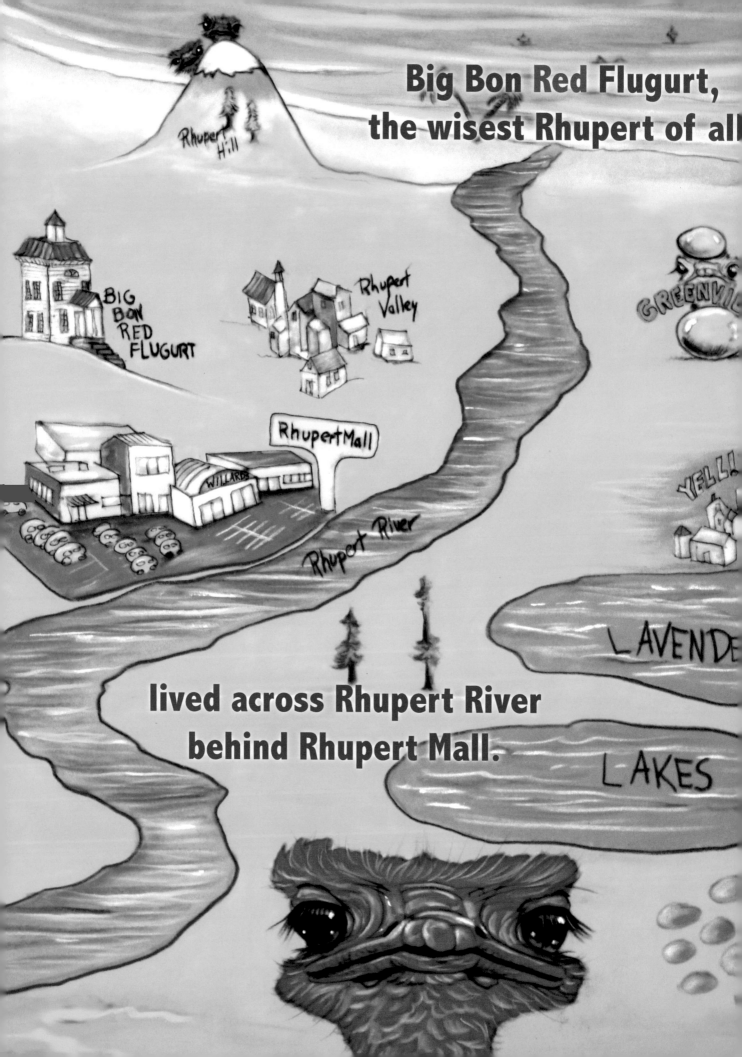

Little Red Rhupert
would ask him,
and ask him he did,

"Why am I so very

different?

Why am I so very

RED?"

Big Bon Red Flugurt sat back in his chair,
stroked his big Rhupert whiskers

and twizzled his hair.

He pondered a moment,
and he lifted his brow;

He started to grin, then he laughed right

OUT
LOUD!

He said,
"Little Red Rhupert, if only you knew,
all the Rhuperts who live here . . .

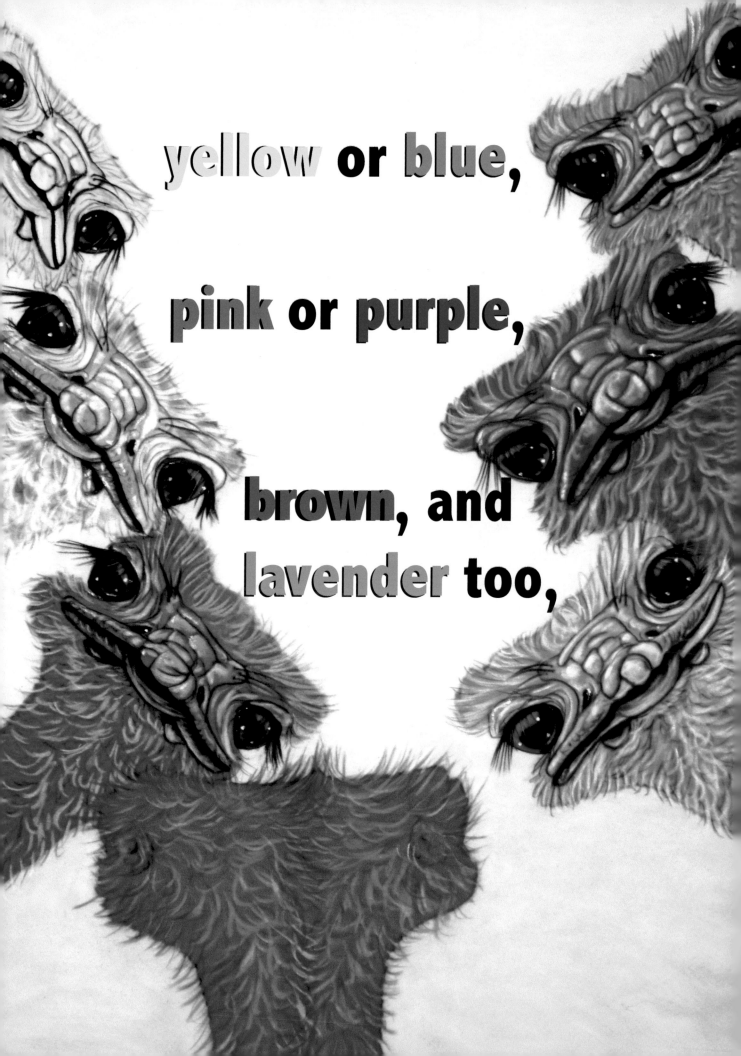

yellow or blue,

pink or purple,

brown, and
lavender too,

even green **Rhuperts**
have all sat in
that chair

asking, 'Why am I so different?'
and in asking they dare...

to see the

TRUTH
underneath
all their plume
and their color,

that we are all still
just Rhuperts,
not much different than the other.

SO, YOU SEE!
SO, YOU SEE!
We've all felt quite the same.
We fit in because we're Rhuperts,

and Rhupert is your NAME."

THE

END

For Seth and Hope:
May beloved community be yours.

GOD'S BELOVED COMMUNITY

Text copyright © 2022 by Michelle T. Sanchez
Cover art and interior illustrations
copyright © 2022 by Camila Carrossine

Published in the United States by WaterBrook,
an imprint of Random House, a division of
Penguin Random House LLC.

WATERBROOK® and its deer colophon are registered
trademarks of Penguin Random House LLC.

ISBN 978-0-593-19388-4
Ebook ISBN 978-0-593-19389-1

The Library of Congress catalog record is available at
https://lccn.loc.gov/2021050852.

Printed in China

waterbrookmultnomah.com

10 9 8 7 6 5 4 3 2 1

First Edition

Book and cover design by Ashley Tucker
Author photo by Duron Studio Photography
Illustrator photo by Alê Camargo

SPECIAL SALES Most WaterBrook books are available
at special quantity discounts when purchased in bulk
by corporations, organizations, and special-interest
groups. Custom imprinting or excerpting can also be
done to fit special needs. For information, please email
specialmarketscms@penguinrandomhouse.com.

GOD'S BELOVED COMMUNITY

WRITTEN BY
Michelle T.
Sanchez

ILLUSTRATED BY
Camila
Carrossine

WATERBROOK

One snowy day, when I was at school,
we learned of Martin Luther King.
We heard him speak a **courageous** dream
with the power to change everything.

Some say Pastor King's dream was color-blind,
ignoring our eyes, hair, and skin,
and looking only at what's inside,
the content of character within.

But at church, we learned his dream was **bigger**,
that Jesus can set us all free
to be not color-blind but **color-brave**,
a beloved community.

You see, Pastor King **believed** in God,
a God made completely of love,
who's writing a story more colorful
than anything we could think of.

Before the beginning, God was three-in-one,
not floating all lonesome in space.
God was Father, Son, and Holy Spirit,
beloved community **already in place.**

And one day God said, "Though this is fun,
I want to embrace so many more."
So God began to spill out his love
in a beautiful **love downpour!**

God birthed a creation full of delight,
diverse in every way,
brimming with vibrant variety:
land and sea, plant and beast, night and day.

Behold colorful crowns of cockatoos.
Look there at flamingos and crows.
See the laughing hyenas, the croaking frogs,
the surprising splash of rainbows!

Look down on the rain-forest canopy,
where margays leap and monkeys swing.
Now look up and—*swoosh!*—a shooting star.
You don't want to miss **anything**.

God laughed and said, "Though this is nice,
what I'd be most proud of
is forming a family a lot like ours
to **expand** this circle of love!"

With that, God formed **Adam** and **Eve**,
the very first woman and man.
God blessed them and bid them to multiply
his love throughout the land.

But that's when love's enemy entered the scene:
a snake who steals, kills, and destroys,
who tries to divide God's beloved community
and rob it of **color**, **peace**, and **joy**.

The snake said, "Listen, you won't die
if you eat fruit from the forbidden tree.
God doesn't love you—you can't trust God!
So put your trust in me."

And, oh, they did! And community broke!
But, of course, our God wasn't done.
He planned to **restore his family of love**
through God's one and only Son.

God gently and patiently started to shape
a new community in his hands.
He showed them what love was really like
in the form of his good commands.

Though the people failed again and again,
God remained **faithful** and **true**.
For the dream of beloved community,
well, there's nothing our God won't do!

God kept forming a people of faith,
ready to spread God's love to the world,
a people on call to break down the walls
between every tribe and tongue, boy and girl.

And then one day **it happened**:
the world met God's own Son!
Jesus came preaching forgiveness to all
and a kingdom big enough for everyone.

Our God loves the world so much
that he seeks out and saves the lost.
In Jesus, God showed the depths of his love
by dying for us on the cross.

So what does this mean for God's people?
It means we're called to do the same:
we are called to lay down our lives
for one another in Jesus's name.

Now, even though we follow Jesus,
we don't always get it right.
Instead of enjoying our **colorful differences**,
we choose to fear and fight.

Rather than loving those who are different
and treating all with care and grace,
we treat some people better than others
simply because of race.

The enemy of love still tries
to destroy and steal and kill,
but in Christ we can always overcome,
for God's love is **stronger** still!

No matter how different your neighbors may be,
even if they seem like enemies,
Jesus gives us the power to bless everyone
and build beloved community.

Friends, no matter how old or young,
like Pastor King, we can be **color-brave**.
We can notice how precious all colors are,
and we can show others the way.

We can learn what makes each color unique
and seek to include everyone.
If you see friends who are getting left out,
you can invite them to join in the fun!

Stand up when you see bullying;
speak out against rules that are unfair.
Declare that **everyone matters** to God!
You can help others to care.

And as you love others like this,
guess what? You make God smile!
Because God's dream is coming true through **you**,
this dream of love he's had for quite a while.

When you reconcile people to God
and to each other as a diverse family,
you spread the good news of this colorful dream:
God's beloved community!